Jessica

Love is worth

Hurting for.

AN UNDEFEATED STREAK NOVEL

LAWSON

WRITTEN BY

A.L. Wood

Cover Model Devin Byrd

Photo Credit to Golden Czermak of Furious Fotog

Cover Design to Rachel Olsen of No Sweat Graphics

Editing credit to Wendi Lynn from Ready Set Edit

Lawson Playlist

I hate u, I love u- Gnash

I Took a Pill in Ibiza- Mike Posner

Needed Me- Rhianna

Can't Stop the Feeling- Justin Timberlake

Lowlife- Future & The Weeknd

Missing You- Betty Who

Pillowtalk- Zayn

Darkest Part- Red

Everything- Bridge to Grace

Gamblin' Man- Smashing Satellites

Only Son- Shakey Graves

Dear Love- Lauren Marsh

River- Bishop Briggs

Tennessee Whiskey- Chris Stapleton

Lost and Alone- From Ashes to New

For the courageous ones who aren't afraid to love wholeheartedly, even if its unrequited.

Lawson

"Tell me you feel it too," Griffin argues with me.

"I'm sorry, I wish I could tell you that I love you, but I don't. Not in the way that you want me to, anyway," I confess, feeling blinded that I never saw this coming

My best friend of over twenty years is in love with me. I didn't know he liked men to begin with, much less *loved* one.

"I've loved you my whole life with all of me; I've stayed here only because of you. If you really don't feel like I do, then I have no other reason to remain. I'll be gone by the morning," Griffin says as he walks away from me and into his room.

I catch his arm before he can make his escape. "You don't have to leave, this changes nothing between us. You're still my best friend, Grif, I love you like a brother. Fuck! You're family, no doubt. I'm sorry that I'm hurting you, but it's just not that way for me."

"We can't go back to that, not after this. Don't lie to yourself—knowing that I love you changes things for us. We'll never have that. I could've shut my mouth, but it was killing me being around you while having to lie to you and myself about my feelings, about who I am. I'm not going to stay, because if I do, every day I am around you I'll regret ever telling you my truth. I can't pretend this never happened, that I don't feel like this. I've tried, and it doesn't work. In time, I will be okay." With that, Griffin slams the door.

Griffin and I grew up together—we were practically born to be best friends. Twenty years of friendship reduced to this: unexpected, unrequited love. I never, *ever* saw this coming. Griff fucked women, lots of women all the time. I'm not biased against men loving men, or shit, anyone loving anyone.

Everyone deserves love.

Griffin deserves love.

But that love isn't me.

CHAPTER ONE

After

"You're picking Sam up from school today, right?" I confirm with Jade before leaving to go to the gym for the day.

"Bain's busy doing some promotional thing you set up, so yeah, I'm grabbing her. I do have to work tonight, though, so if he isn't home by her bedtime, is there any way you can sit over there until he or Rumer show?"

"Not a problem, just give me a call and I'll be there. See ya tonight." Kissing her on the forehead, I leave.

***

"Please don't admit that you're so oblivious that you don't see how in love with you she is ..."

Looking to the newest member of my gym while she approaches a treadmill, I say, "Fuck off, Sean, she's in lust. Definitely not love."

"Nope. I'm telling you, she's in love. She's a regular groupie around here. She doesn't even work out; I don't know why she even bothers paying for a gym membership when every time she shows up she leaves right away if she doesn't see you. She only stays when you're here," Sean argues.

"Wrong." He's off the mark here. Sure, I've seen her a couple times already this week and maybe a few last week, but she's not once said a word to me. She hasn't hinted at any type of interest; she hasn't even looked my way.

"Am not. Who'd pay fifty bucks a month for a lay? Who would spend that gas money let alone that much time coming here every fucking day? Lust? No, love. Love does that."

"You're biased because you're a romantic at heart and also the blind one. You can't tell the difference between love and lust. I pity the fuck out of the woman who doesn't want a relationship with you. I can see it now, she just wants a lay and you profess your love. She'll ditch you as fast as she can because she'll label you a clinger."

"One, it won't be a woman because I love me some man. Two, mark my words, she wants you, and she wants you for more than one night. She might not be the final one for you, but she'll take up some of your time until you find that one. When you do come across the girl that's it, you're going to miss her because you're so caught up in being alone. Try not to make that mistake, 'cause once you lose your final, she won't be coming back."

"Man, woman, you'll confuse lust and love all the same, and I won't miss my one and only, because there isn't one. I only have a one-for-the-night."

"Keep thinking like that, we'll see who's right. In fact, we'll see soon," Sean says, looking over my shoulder. "She's headed our way now. I'll give you some privacy."

"I don't need privacy, don't go," I say, but he's already walked away.

I head over to the weight benches, picking up sanitizer and some paper towels on my way, hoping she'll keep walking by me when she sees that I'm busy cleaning.

Of course, though, she stops to tap me on my shoulder. I set the towels and sanitizer down, and ask politely, "Can I help you with something?" I do own the gym, and she's a customer, so it's only the right way to act.

"Actually, you can. I couldn't help but notice that you're here every time I'm here. I don't normally do this, but I was wondering if you wanted to go out this weekend?"

You see me here every time you're here because I own the gym, I want to say, but I don't. It wouldn't be polite.

"I don't want to lead you on, but normally I don't do the dating thing. I'm not looking for a relationship."

"I wasn't asking you to marry me. I find you attractive, so I thought maybe we could hang out, see where the night took us. You do have friends, right? If you wanted, you could invite them, we can do a double date or something. Get one of your buddies to tag along, he can protect your virtue." She laughs.

"All right. You sold me, but you can't say that I didn't warn you," I give in easily. I'm human, I have needs. Needs that I generally neglect because I'm always so damn busy. One date can't hurt, especially when I warned her that I wasn't looking to get into anything serious.

"How's dinner sound?"

"Sounds great, leave your address at the desk with Sean, and I'll get it from him later. I'll pick you up Friday at seven."

"Okay, I'll see you then."

CHAPTER TWO

Jade

"Hey, Sammy, how was school today?" I ask as she climbs into the backseat of my car.

"Fine," she grumbles out.

"What's wrong?"

"Nothing. I'm okay, can we just go home?"

"You know that you can tell me anything, right? I'll always be here for you. Whenever you want to talk about what happened today, you can come to me."

"I know; I just want to go home. Will Dad be there soon?"

"I'm not sure, he didn't say when he'd be home. I have to work tonight, so if he or Rumer aren't home by then, Lawson will be with you."

"Okay. Can I help you make dinner then?"

"Sure. What did you want to make?"

"Do you still have any of those chicken nuggets left? The ones that look like dinosaurs? They're my favorite. I want to make those."

"Yeah, I have some of those left still. Chicken nuggets and fries for dinner, how's that sound?"

"Yummy!"

I grab my purse then slide out of my car to open Sam's door. Following me up the stairs, she grabs my hand. "Promise you won't tell Dad?"

"I can't make that promise, Sammy, if it's something that can harm you or someone else I have to tell Dad."

"It's nothing like that."

"Okay, then I promise. Come on in and tell Aunt Jade all of your problems."

Swinging the door open, she flies past me and jumps on the couch.

"It's this girl, Tiffany. She's in my class, and she keeps asking about my mom. Not Rumer, but my *real* mom, the one who isn't here. I don't want to tell Tiffany because I don't think it's her business, but she keeps saying that my mom isn't around because she didn't love me. Is that true?"

"Samantha …" I pause, collecting my thoughts before replying. I want children of my own, I always have; I have always known that I'm a maternal sort of person. I am a nurturer, but children like Tiffany make me question reproducing. What if I created a human being that was so heartless? As a parent, I wouldn't able to be there all of the time, I wouldn't be able to make sure they're acting with kindness and compassion. I would have to instill those morals and character traits while raising my child and pray for the best.

I've never met Tiffany, so she must be a newer student. I don't know if her parents are just as heartless and maybe that's where she got it from. I don't know what that seven-year-old child's story is, but saying something like this to Samantha is completely uncalled for and hurtful. I want to call her school right now and demand they give me the number to Tiffany's parents, but that won't help Samantha at this moment. "What Tiffany said is not true. Your mother loved you very much. She didn't go away because of you or anyone else. An accident happened that stole her from all of us. I know that if she could have been here with you, watching you grow, she would be. She would have wanted that so bad, but we can't change that. You do not have to tell Tiffany where your Mom is or what happened to her— you're right, it is none of her business. Rumer or I will never take your Mom's place, but we will always be here for you, forever. You are ours, and you are loved."

She's crying by the time I say the last word. "I love you guys too."

"Come here and give me a hug." Sam leans in to me, and I hold her.

I hold her for a few minutes then wipe the last remnants of tears from my eyes. "Hungry? We can make dinner." I smile down at her.

"Yeah, I'm hungry."

I yank the frozen, dinosaur-shaped chicken nuggets out of the freezer and the bag of seasoned fries. "I should really stop buying this crap, it's not good for us. If Lawson or your father were to walk in to find us eating this, our ears would be bleeding from the lecture we'd receive on how unhealthy this stuff is, so you better keep this a secret."

"As long as you keep buying it, I won't say anything."

CHAPTER THREE

Lawson

Running my fingers through my short brown hair, I realize the amount of paperwork I have done and have yet to do tonight are too much. My eyes are hurting, and every word and number are bleeding together on the page. I should really get Jade in here a couple of times a month to manage the books for me; it would be one less shift at the bar she'd take.

Woman doesn't even need money; don't know why she does it anymore. Thinking of the devil, my cell starts ringing. "Yeah?"

"Any way you can come sit with Sam? Bain and Rumer aren't back yet, and I have to make it to the bar by ten," Jade pleads.

"I'll be there in a couple."

"Thanks."

I shut my computer off, lock my office, and leave the gym. Sean is a newer hire who passed a complete background check—I know that I can leave my gym in his hands and it will be okay. I hired him because I knew that with Bain's notoriety and our travel and training schedule there was no way I could be there every open hour, beyond staying late to account for every penny. It just wasn't possible.

I offered the job to Jade first since she knew the gym inside and out. She is aware of how I like everything ran, when to open, when to close, and how every piece of equipment should be cleaned. She also knew how to manage my accounts; she was an asset I couldn't live without. She agreed to help with the books when I needed it without pay but turned down my job offer because of the fucking bar. She even had the audacity to accuse me of making up an unneeded fake job just to get her away from there. She knows now that I was one hundred percent serious because she met Sean, my second choice.

In all seriousness, I would've made up any job to get her away from that place. I've tried it before, and I will try it again—she's too good for that seedy place. She thinks that I have no clue what goes on there, that I'm not made aware of how she's overworked and harassed, but I am. I have eyes wherever she goes, always making sure she's protected and okay whenever I can't be around.

Jade and I grew up together, she and I have always been friends, but we became best friends when Griffin left. She became my roommate eight years ago not because I needed one, but because I didn't like living alone. In those eight years, she'd brought up moving out three times, all because she was in a serious relationship that she wanted to take up a notch.

All three times gutted me, made me a ridiculously jealous asshole—even though I'm not nor have ever been interested in her that way. Each time, she's always stayed because she felt like I needed her more than she needed a relationship.

Maybe the fourth time will be the time she leaves.

CHAPTER FOUR

Jade

"That was fast," I greet Lawson at the door.

"You called, I came."

"I called an hour early because usually you take forever and I have to actually be on time tonight. Someone rented out the entire bar for a bachelor party, and I'm stuck prepping for the shindig."

"Come work for me," he begs, again.

"You know that I can't."

"You keep saying that you can't, but never actually give me a reason as to why. So tell me now, why?"

Because I love you.

"It would never work, Lawson. We live together, we cook together, we eat together, we do everything together! I need space away from you sometimes. I need things that are just for me, not for Jade and Lawson."

He steps back, his face tight and held in a grimace as if I offended him. "I didn't know you felt that way."

"I didn't mean it the way you're taking it. All I'm saying is that we're around each other all the time. I can't see myself working with you and not wanting to harm you. It's not healthy to always be with someone all of the time. You know I love being around you; you're my best friend. I just need some me time."

"Fine, I'll stop bugging you about your job for a while. If you won't work with me then I'd rather you at least apply somewhere else, *any*where else. Please consider it?"

"Deal." Remembering I have less than an hour to clock in, I update Lawson, "Sam didn't have a great day at school today, so she's a little upset. We had dinner, and she's in the living room watching the movie with those silly yellow creatures. Rumer sent me a text right before you got here; they should be home in two hours. Just keep her entertained, will ya?"

"You know she's always entertained around me. I'm her favorite uncle, after all."

"Okay, I have to get dressed for work. I'll be home late so don't wait up."

"Oh, hey, before I forget, did you want to go on a double date Friday night? I was asked out today at the gym, and she suggested I bring a friend along. I wasn't sure if you had anyone in mind to invite, but you could always come alone if you don't."

"Umm yeah, I guess … I could … Umm, maybe," I stumble on my words. *Get it together.* Smoothing my hands over my shirt, I build up the courage to tell Lawson my second ever bold-faced lie, "Sure. I've had my eye on someone anyway. I'll ask him if he wants to go on a double date. He'll probably say yes, so yeah, just plan for us to join you."

"Who?"

"Excuse me?"

"Who have you had your eyes on? Who are you bringing? Do I know him? You're either here, at the gym, or at work, so I know you haven't had time to go out and meet anyone. Who is he?" Lawson grumbles.

"What's with the twenty questions? He's a guy from work, don't worry about it."

"Don't worry? How could I not worry? You're like my sister for fuck's sake. I don't want you dating someone who doesn't deserve you, J."

Sister, just like your sister. "You worry too much. Anyway, I have to get ready."

"Yeah, yeah. I've got Sam, go get dressed, and remember your pepper spray."

"Got it, Dad," I joke.

After getting the entire bar decorated for a bachelor party—a perverted bachelor party—I'm able to take a quick fifteen-minute break before having to stand behind the bar for the next four hours in heels while getting hit on by single *and* married men. I choose to spend my break outside, enjoying the fresh air while thinking about what Lawson had said earlier.

He's going on a date—scratch that, he's going on a date and wants me and my date of choice to tag along.

Lawson never, *ever* goes on dates.

The guy that I was consumed with love for was going on his first actual date, one that wasn't with me. As in, he wasn't going on the date with me and me alone as his love interest.

Oh, I was going, but as his best friend, someone he sees as his *sister*.

I don't know why I keep doing this to myself.

Loving him from afar, him oblivious to my feelings, not seeing the pain I go through as he waltzes through life from one woman to the next never being in a relationship. He doesn't see how me loving him causes me to suffer.

There are times I can't breathe while being in the same room as him for fear that I won't be able to restrain myself from confessing, from touching him.

Lawson going on a date only means one thing.

I will never be her. I'll never be *his*.

It's time that I move on. Time to grow up and find someone who will love me as I love him.

"Ready for tonight?" Jax asks, pulling me from my thoughts.

"As ready as I'll ever be. I'm glad you came out here before the madness. I wanted to ask you if you wanted to join me for dinner Friday night. It's with a friend and his date. You don't have to, though, if you don't want to."

"Will we be on a date too?"

I feel my face heat up, blushing. I've never asked anyone out; it was always the other way around. "If you want it to be a date I wouldn't complain," I flirt.

"It's a date then. Friday night. What time?"

Shit, I had forgotten to ask Lawson. "I'll let you know before I leave tonight."

"I can't wait."

He goes back inside so I use that moment to send Lawson a text before the house gets crazy.

Me: He said yes. What time was dinner and where? I can ride with him and meet you and your date at the restaurant.

He replies immediately.

Lawson: Seven. You're riding with me, though; he can meet us at Mido Mio.

Me: I'll be on a date with him, not you so I can ride with him. Plus, I'm sure your date wouldn't appreciate another woman in the car, double date or not.

Lawson: I don't like this Jade. I've never even met who you're bringing, I can't just trust him with you.

Me: You don't have to trust him, he's not dating you.

Lawson: I still don't like it. He better have you there at seven or I will come looking for you.

Me: Yes dad.

Lawson: I'm not your father.

No, you're right, you're my "brother."

Me: Yes brother. Have to go back in, busy night. See you tomorrow.

Lawson: I'll be up.

CHAPTER FIVE

Lawson

Three in the morning, and she still isn't home. I hate that she works so late, not just because of the place, but the idea of her walking out to her car this late at night all alone makes me uncomfortable. No one else has ever affected me like Jade. With her, I always feel like I'm responsible for her well-being. I want to see her happy and be the reason she's feeling such joy. I like knowing that she's always a room down from me so that if anything were to happen I was only feet away.

I don't like knowing that some other knucklehead will be bringing her on a date, someone I haven't had the chance to meet or get a background check on. Fuck! I don't even know his name. She has to tell me his name.

Me: What's his name?

Jade: I'm at work and it's a mad house, stop texting me and go to bed.

Me: I'll stop texting you if you just tell me his name.

Jade: His name is Jax. Good night.

Me: Jax what? I need his full name, and if you can his address.

Jade: Are you kidding me Law? No. I am not telling you his last name, nor will I be giving you his address. I don't even know where he lives. Forget him, he isn't your concern. You will not be running a background check on him. I don't need to know all of his secrets, if he has any. It would be his place to tell me if he and I get serious. Not yours, so stop thinking about it and go to sleep.

Me: Well talk about this when you get home.

I don't go to sleep. Instead, knowing that Samantha has already gone to bed, I head over to Bain and Rumer's place.

"So, let me get this straight, you agreed to go on a date with a member of your gym. Something you've never done, and to top it off, you're having Jade bring a date with her to yours?"

"Well, when you say it like that, it does sound kind of messed up, but yeah."

"You shouldn't have invited Jade. Rumer and I would've gladly gone, but this isn't something you should've brought her into."

"It's not like she doesn't go on dates."

"No, but I'm sure this isn't something she'd be comfortable with, but now it's done, so you have to roll with the punches. Make it a quick outing, don't go to the movies or something. Just food."

"I already had that planned, we're just going to dinner. Anyway, that's not why I came over. What's really bugging me is that she's bringing some guy from work. You know how I feel about that place and generally the people there aren't like Jade."

"It's not as bad of a place as you make it out to be. You never gave it or her working there a chance because you have her on some untouchable pedestal. She's a grown woman; you can't tell her where to work or what to do just because you don't like it. You need to get over this already."

"Logically, I know that I have no say, and I shouldn't even feel like I do. I just want better for her, that's all."

"Well, maybe this date thing could be good. You can finally find someone to occupy your time. That way, you won't have the free time to worry about everything Jade's doing."

"I don't know, maybe you're right."

"You'll see. All right, long day tomorrow, so you need to go back to your own place."

"Yeah, yeah."

"Night."

"Yup."

CHAPTER SIX

Jade

Tossing my keys on the table, I slip my shoes off and make my way to the refrigerator for a bottled water. Tonight felt like it took forever to get through—it was one thing after another. The bachelor of the party was the worst, constantly groping the waitresses. Thankfully, I was well hidden behind the bar tonight, but not everyone was so lucky. Not only were his hands wandering, he lit one of his drinks on fire with a damn candle lighter, which is against the rules no matter how much he paid to rent the entire bar out. Only a bartender can do that because we have a fire extinguisher right below the counter. Fool.

All of the bachelor's friends were in their mid-thirties but had you entered the bar tonight you would've thought they all just turned twenty-one and that it was their first night drinking. It was exhausting, to say the least.

Tipping the water bottle back to drink the cold refreshing liquid, I open my mouth, salivating at the feel of ice-cold water when two hands are placed on my sides.

"Boo!"

The water ends up splashing on my face and down my chin, then eventually all over my shirt. "Fucking hell! Why would you do that?"

"I wanted to scare you?" Lawson raises his eyebrows as if it wasn't a statement but a question.

"Do you know what time it is? You were supposed to be in bed. I thought you were a robber or something. You don't sneak up on someone at four in the morning while they're trying to take a drink all just to scare them. You're lucky I didn't punch you or something."

"Jade, you'd never hit me. Even if you tried, I'd block you before you could reach me. Anyway, I told you I'd be up. We need to talk."

I set my water on the counter, walk to the wall, and switch the light on. If he insists we have to have this conversation, it isn't going to be in the dark; it's going to be in the light where I can see his face clearly so that I can try to read him and his emotions.

I used to never be able to tell how he was feeling or what he was thinking—his emotions were always held on lock down as tight as a fortress. Since I moved in, though, I've been able to read him. Over the years, I've gotten better at it.

It's how I know that he'll never feel the same way about me as I feel about him.

He's never given me a look of desire or interest. No, the look reserved for me—and always me—was one of brotherly love, like he had an obligation to protect me. The women that are in and out of his bed and never the same woman twice, those are the ones who get the bedroom eyes, the caress from his lips, the feel of his muscular body over them all night long.

Boy, do I know it.

I fucking hear it.

It's the reason I went out and bought noise canceling headphones. It was killing me inside to know that I would never feel him in that way, that I would never receive his attention in the way that I wished I would.

No.

I would never know what it was like to be cherished and loved by Lawson.

"You've got me. Speak," I say shortly, wanting to get this conversation over with. It's bad enough I agreed to go out on a double date, his first date ever. Sitting through that meal is going to be the death of me.

I wish I could just turn the love I have for him off, just like I turned the light on. A simple flick of the switch would heal me. If only it worked that way.

"I just wanted you to give me his name. I get it if you don't want to give me his address. I wouldn't if I were you; you know me too damn well. I don't even want his address anymore—if I knew it, I would be tempted to visit him, check his place out. See what kind of person he is. Just give me his name so I can at least make sure he's not some criminal, J. You can't say no to that. I need to know that you'll be okay with him alone. Please."

"Fine, his name is Jax Roman. Look him up. I'm going to bed. I'm exhausted, and I had a long night. Goodnight, Law."

"Night, J."

CHAPTER SEVEN

Lawson

"Over here," I call out to Jade as she and her date exit his vehicle.

Mido Mio is this small Italian restaurant situated on a corner in downtown Philly that offers inside seating as well as outside.

Shay and I chose to sit outside so that Jade and Jax could easily locate us. Besides, the evening isn't too warm. It is a perfect evening for a date under the stars.

"You didn't tell me your buddy was a woman," Shay complains, jealous tinging her every word.

"Correction, she's my best buddy and she brought a date."

Jax pulls the chair across from me out so that Jade can sit, and after pushing her in, he seats himself.

"Lawson, and this is Shay. Shay, this is Jade and Jax." I make the introductions so that there isn't any awkward silence. It's bad enough I'm out on a date in the first place.

My first date.

I continue, "I thought we could do the five-course plate; you can choose something from each category, but unless you've all been here before, it would be a good way to sample the menu and fill up."

"Sounds good to me," Jade agrees easily. Jax and Shay agree as well.

The waitress greets us, then takes our order as we were all pretty agreeable when ordering.

I take a sip of my water, Jade does as well.

This entire situation is uncomfortable; I shouldn't have asked her, but I needed some kind of buffer. She's the first person that came to my mind when Shay suggested I bring a friend. Jade has never failed me, in every single situation that I can remember over the last eight years she's kept me calm, collected. I'm not a nervous person, I just like having someone that can always ground me.

Jade keeps my feet rooted to the floor with ease. No one else has been able to do this, not even Griffin.

It's been silent since our order was taken, and I assume it'll be a little while before our first course is served. Deciding to break the quiet, I pull Jade with me into conversation, hoping that it will lift the tension I'm consumed with. "You never told me how the bachelor party went."

"That's because you never asked. It was absolute hell."

"You need to take my advice and just quit."

Jax adds his input, "I don't think I've seen a bachelor party go from great to so bad as fast as this one did. Jade was harassed all night."

This earns Jade an eyebrow raise. I will definitely be asking her about this when we get home tonight.

"It was nothing that I haven't experienced before while working there, I promise. It was just a couple of drunk guys hitting on the bartender hoping to score some free drinks. Harmless, really," she tries to reason with me.

"Doesn't matter, that place isn't safe for someone like you."

Shit. Foot meet mouth.

"Someone like me? What's that supposed to mean?"

"How well do you two know each other?" Shay asks.

I ignore her. Jade is more important. She's pissed, and I have to calm her before a simple comment becomes an argument all night long.

"Jade, listen to reason, please. I've been practically begging you to just leave that place. You refused my job offer, and that's all fine and dandy, but there's a lot of jobs out there that you could apply for. Great jobs that don't involve you being harassed. What if one guy takes it too far? You're barely five feet five and weigh at the most one hundred and thirty pounds. You've got muscle, I'll give you that, but you don't have the knowledge of defense.

Someone could easily overtake you and you're down to be taken advantage of. I don't want that shit, I worry about you enough as it is. Not to mention the late hours you work. I want to see you doing something better with your life. Fuck, you don't even need a job, and you know that."

Jade remains silent.

Jax with his eyes wide open staring at me tells me that I probably pushed her too far. Shay steps on my foot below the table. Apparently, I'm the asshole outcast tonight.

Did I go too far? *Maybe.*

I might've just told her earlier this week that I would stop pushing the issue about her work, I could've even promised. Maybe I would've kept that promise if she didn't hide the shit that goes on down there, if she just told me the truth about it all the time.

"Lawson, I do not need your Alpha bullshit laying at my feet. I am a grown woman; I know how to defend myself. Unbeknownst to you, I've taken a class or two on that. Just because you weren't my teacher does not mean that I cannot protect my own self. You are not my father, nor are you my boyfriend. You are my friend. That's it. You have no say in how I spend my time, so I would appreciate it if you would drop the subject. Now, if you would all excuse me, I have to go to the restroom." She pushes her chair out and makes her way into the restaurant.

"I fucked up, didn't I?" I ask Jax and Shay. They both nod their heads. "I'll be right back."

Knocking on the restroom door, I plead, "Jade, let me in for a minute."

"I'm going to the bathroom, go away."

She's lying. I can hear the broken shakiness in her voice—she's crying.

"Stop lying, just unlock the door and let me in or I'll make a scene."

I hear the lock click so I open the door only to find her leaning against the sink wiping her eyes with a tissue.

I meet her back with my chest, and, looking into the mirror, I catch her eyes. "I'm sorry."

"You humiliated me. We've talked about this just the other day and many times before. This is my job, and I chose it. You don't get to have a say about it, yet you always have to voice your opinions like I should be doing exactly as you say. You don't have that right. Then you decide to bring this up on my first date with Jax? That's fucked up, Law."

"I know, I know. It's just that every time I think about you working there I get this sick feeling in my gut, and it doesn't sit well with me. I didn't mean to humiliate you, please forgive me."

"As long as you promise not to do it again and you keep your opinions to yourself when I'm on a date. I like him, so don't ruin my chance."

Just hearing her say that she likes him burns me from the inside out. What does he have that deserves her liking him? Is this really their first date, or has she had some secret relationship with him for a while? I mean, going on your first date and declaring some likeness is too sudden, right?

Right?

"Like him?"

She smiles. "Yeah, I like him. He's kind, likes the same kind of music I do, and he's attractive."

The ugly beast Jealousy rears its head. "Then you could say the same things about me."

"It's not the same, Lawson, you're my best friend, not my lover," she whispers.

"Are you and this guy fucking?" I spit out, needing her to tell me the truth. The idea of her fucking this guy … I don't know why but it doesn't feel right. He shouldn't get to feel her smooth skin, to taste her perfectly-plump pink lips. He shouldn't get to run his fingers through her hair, or grip her ass as he wraps her legs around him. He gets to be that lucky.

"That's none of your business."

"The fuck it is. I'm your best friend, right?"

"We're not having this conversation. Let's get back to dinner and see if you can repair the damage you've done."

I can't do that, not at this moment. I have to hope that he hasn't tasted her sweet lips yet, but just in case he has, I ask, "Fuck it, does he kiss you like this?"

CHAPTER EIGHT

Jade

I attempt to ask Lawson what he means by that, but my words are muffled when one of his hands clutch the back of my neck and the other grips my waist as his lips descend to mine. He doesn't do the sweet and slow thing— no, he's unadulterated heat. His lips take mine roughly, his tongue demanding entrance as the hand on my waist sweeps around and down to my ass. His fingers grip me, pulling me into him. All the while, I can't deny everything that he's asked of me with his lips and fingers.

I want this.

Oh, how I've wanted this for so long.

Almost my entire life I have dreamt of this very moment, I have longed for him to kiss me. To feel how my heart pounds whenever I'm in his presence, for him to feel how much I need him when he takes me and makes me his.

Out of nowhere, I moan, and my hands press against his chest. Not as a means to push him away but to feel him. To finally feel him. I glide my hands down his torso, memorizing every single dip and ridge. I kiss him back again and again as he lifts my legs and shoves me against the wall.

My skirt rises on its own accord, his bulge rubbing against my panties, and I'm forced back into reality. If I give myself to him, it will not be in the public bathroom of a restaurant. No, it will be in his bed, at home. *Our* home.

I shove Lawson away, and he easily loosens his hold on me before my feet drop to the floor. My chest heaving, I breathe in and out slowly. Lawson kissing me was an emotional overthrow. It was almost too much.

I meet his eyes, about to tell him that if we are to go further it will be at home.

About to confess my love.

"I-I—"

Lawson cuts me off, "I'm sorry." He looks away, ashamed. Mortified.

Oh.

Oh.

Oh, my God.

What have I done? What did I almost do? Of course he's sorry, because he doesn't feel the same way that I do. Because all that I am and all that I will ever be is nothing more than just his best friend.

Don't let him see. You're okay. You will be okay.

"I don't know what came over me. I didn't mean to kiss you, J. You have to know that, you're my best friend. Can we pretend it never happened? Please," he begs me to forget.

Those words break my heart.

Loving your best friend from afar isn't so hard to live with when said friend never dates and rarely has female interactions. Loving your best friend isn't hard when you live with him. Loving your best friend isn't hard when you know that in his own way he loves you too. Loving your best friend isn't hard when you've never confessed your love. Loving your best friend isn't hard when you've never kissed.

Loving your best friend is so damn hard when you kiss only to find out after they regret that kiss. Loving your best friend is so damn hard when you're not the one they're going out on a date with. Loving your best friend is the worst when he doesn't love you.

"Sure, it never happened. My lips are sealed."

CHAPTER NINE

Lawson

What have I done?

I had to apologize, I never meant to kiss her. I didn't want to let her believe I was interested in her in that way, that she and I would cross over from friends to lovers or something. Women always over-analyze, always make something out of nothing, so I wanted to prevent that.

I am aware that Jade isn't a normal woman, but I had to make sure she wouldn't read into the kiss we shared.

"Sure, it never happened. My lips are sealed."

That's what Jade had said, and as I leave Shays house from dropping her off, it's all I keep replaying in my head.

Knowing that Bain is home, I decide to skip my apartment door and head down to his, needing him to tell me what I did was wrong. I skip knocking—we grew up together and have lived next door to each other for years; the knocking stopped becoming a thing when we were kids.

I swing the door open and call out to him.

"Early date night," he comments.

"Yeah, have to get up early so I just dropped her off home. Told her I'd give her a call for another date."

"Okay, one date and I was suspicious. You've never gone out on a damn date. A second date tells me that my suspicion that something is going on was right. So, tell me, what's up?"

"That's why I'm here. The date didn't go too well, she wanted me to bring a friend and I'm thinking I should've brought someone besides Jade."

"I doubt she was talking about your best girl buddy, but go on."

"I don't know dude; I couldn't help myself tonight. Jade brought her co-worker as her date, some douchewad who didn't look at all her type, and for some reason, it irritated me so I brought up how I didn't like her working there, how I wished she would find some other job."

"I take it that didn't go over well."

"Not at all. She bugged, she didn't go apeshit or anything. She kept her cool while glaring at me, but like I said, I couldn't stop myself. She finally had enough and excused herself from the table. By that point, Jax and Shay both knew I had upset her, so I followed her so I could apologize. Made her unlock the bathroom door to let me in, then I fucking kissed her."

Bain remains silent. Letting the news that I kissed Jade hang in the air between us.

Moments later, he regains his voice to say, "Finally."

"Excuse me?"

"About fucking time you manned up and kissed her. She's been waiting forever."

"What?" I growl out.

What is he talking about?

"You've got to know that woman has been in love with you since she was a girl."

"I'm being serious here, I messed up. I shouldn't have kissed her."

"I'm being serious too, she's been in love with you for forever. You kissing her was the best choice you've made in a while. Now, go home and kiss her some more so I can go kiss my woman. Don't know what your damn problem is."

"I am not kissing her again, it was a mistake, and you're wrong—Jade isn't in love with me. I'm like her damn brother, family almost. She and I kissing will not happen again, I already asked her to forget it happened. She agreed. I just came over because I wasn't sure how to proceed."

"You proceed with kissing her again. That girl is yours. She's right for you, dude. She puts up with your shit, never backs down. Takes care of your miserable ass, nurses you when you're sick, and does your damn laundry. She's practically your live-in wife already, the only thing you haven't done is consummated the marriage. Asking her to pretend it didn't happen is most likely only going to cause you hell."

"She's not my wife. Roommates who are best friends take care of each other, that's all we are. She's someone's for sure, just not mine. What do you think's going to happen by pretending a kiss never happened?"

"She's going to be hurt, that's for sure, because she loves you. I've known it for years, don't know how you've ignored it but I'm telling you, kissing her and then dismissing it like it was nothing just messed whatever you think you've got with her all up."

Shit.

"How do I fix it?"

"Truth is, I don't know how. Depends on how pissed and hurt she is. She could just be done with your ass and walk away, tired of waiting on you to see the truth. Or she could wallow in that hurt and try to hurt you back. Either way, I would just give her some space. I'm sure she's needing it right now."

Space.

Giving Jade space?

No.

Okay, maybe for one night.

"Can I crash here?"

"I'm not becoming an accomplice for your asshole behavior. You all just went out on a date. You left with your date, you not coming home looks like you stayed the night with that girl after kissing her. Asking her to forget the kiss you gave her, that will hurt her. Kissing her, asking her to forget it, then leaving with your date and not coming home. That shit won't just hurt her; it will break her heart. Go home, Law."

"But maybe it would be easier to break her heart now. If you're right and she does have feelings for me. Maybe I should just hurt her now, save her the pain of thinking something can happen between us."

"It's already happened, Lawson, it's *been* happening. Hurting her now or tomorrow or a week from now won't hurt her any less. You want to play blind? Go ahead, pretend that you've never felt her love. Pretend that you've never seen it. Pretend that you don't need it. But go pretend at your house."

"Night, Bain."

CHAPTER TEN

Jade

You want me to pretend? Sure, I'll go on like I always have been, not that you can tell, apparently. How can someone forget when the person they love finally kisses them? Those few moments when receiving the long-awaited kiss is filled with extreme and restless hope.

I saw our future in those seconds.

I saw what he and I could be, the life we could have. One that was filled with deeply fulfilling love. A love that he clearly does not feel for me, because as soon as we pulled apart he had no problem crushing the future I had seen.

If living with Lawson for years hasn't produced any feelings for me on his part, and a kiss obviously didn't, then nothing will.

I refuse to waste my life feeling love for someone that will never feel the same for me. I'll always love Lawson, and I doubt that I'll find a love so powerful with anyone else but I deserve more.

I have to make a future for myself that doesn't involve him as my lover.

"Even though your friend was a bit rude and you got upset, I still had a good time. Maybe we can do this again but without him?" Jax asks.

I don't want to be that woman, the one who runs to the first guy who shows her attention, the first willing, wanting, and waiting man.

I'm not desperate for anyone's love—I'm desperate for Lawson's love and to run to anyone else while trying to find who I am without loving Lawson isn't fair to myself or anyone else.

It's not fair to Jax to just lead him on when I'll never be fully invested in creating something with him while I'm still not over Lawson.

No matter how much I want to move forward.

"I had a nice time tonight too, and as much as I'd like to go on another date with you, I don't think now is the right time. I'm sorry."

"It's okay, when you feel like it's the time, just give me a call. I'll be there."

"Thank you, Jax. Good night."

"Good night, Jade." He kisses me on my cheek before I exit his car.

I see that Lawson's truck is in the driveway; apparently, he had an early night as well. The way Shay was running her hands all over his body I was sure that he wouldn't be home. Figured he'd be spending the night with her.

It shouldn't give me any type of relief knowing that he dropped her off and came straight home, but it does.

I enter our apartment and am greeted with silence.

"Lawson?" I call out.

Hoping that maybe he and I can talk, come to some sort of agreement with our friendship. I can pretend that our kiss never happened as long as he promises to never do it again. We can't be friends and I can't move on with the thought of it happening again being a possibility. It just gives me false hope.

Lawson doesn't answer so I knock on his bedroom door. Again, no answer, so I open the door to see that he's not there.

Hmmm ... maybe he's next door.

Outside Bain and Rumor's door I can hear Lawson's gruff voice, "Yeah, have to get up early so I just dropped her off home. Told her I'd give her a call for another date."

Of course he would, the one time he goes out on an actual date he falls for the woman. Can't blame him—she was beautiful and seemed more his type than me.

I overhear Bain tell Lawson of his suspicion that something was going on. Like a lurker, I wait to hear his response, because I want to know too. I have to know. Lawson tells him how he never wanted me to go in the first place, but Shay did because she could tell he was uncomfortable. Use me as a buffer, sure.

"I don't know, dude, I couldn't help myself tonight. Jade brought her co-worker as her date, some douchewad who didn't look at all her type, and for some reason, it irritated me, so I brought up how I didn't like her working there, how I wished she would find some other job."

My type is you, you asshole.

Bain predicts that I was upset by Lawson's behavior; I had every right to be. He was full of angst and controlling and wanted to show Jax just how close we were. I felt like he was claiming his territory in words, a warning for Jax to run away because I wasn't to be messed with. Even though Lawson never planned on actually claiming me, which is obvious by wanting to pretend a heated and passionate kiss never existed.

"Not at all. She bugged, she didn't go apeshit or anything. She kept her cool while glaring at me, but like I said, I couldn't stop myself. She finally had enough and excused herself from the table, but by that point, Jax and Shay both knew I had upset her, so I followed her so I could apologize. Made her unlock the bathroom door to let me in, then I fucking kissed her."

Then I fucking kissed her.

I could hear his disgust with himself and me in his voice.

He didn't lie when he said it was a mistake, he wasn't pretending to hide feelings he had deep down. He really meant it.

My stomach bottoms out.

I shouldn't be listening to their conversation.

I should just go back to our apartment and go to bed, pretend that kiss and their conversation never happened.

Curiosity killed the cat and all.

Curiosity was going to kill me.

But I stay anyway.

Because I realize that if I want to move on, I have to allow Lawson to truly hurt me. I can't keep the façade of maybe him coming to his senses and seeing what's been in front of him all along. I can't hold on to that hope anymore, so I stay.

I hear Bain exclaim, "Finally."

Yeah, that's how I felt too.

"Excuse me?"

Lawson didn't feel that way.

"About fucking time you manned up and kissed her, she's been waiting forever."

I could hug you right now, Bain, for being my voice. For encouraging Lawson to see what you see.

"What?" Lawson growls out with disgust.

"You've got to know that woman has been in love with you since she was a girl," Bain barks back.

He's right. Even is Lawson didn't want my love, he had already stolen it when we were kids. We all grew up on the same street, our houses all bunched together on the same block. Griffin, Bain's brother, and Lawson had been best friends already when I met them. Bain and I were in kindergarten, and he was the only person who was nice to me in class.

So I used to follow him everywhere when we were home playing outside, and in turn, Bain would follow Griffin and Lawson around. Girls never wanted to be my friend. It wasn't that I wasn't open to it, because I was. It was that I was best friends with three boys that intimidated girls from even trying to say hello. And that was okay, because why did I need any more friends when I had so many already? Lawson was an instant love for me. My five-year-old mind could see what a kind boy he was, and as we got older, that love only became more real, and not for childish reasons but adult, womanly reasons.

He never saw it because I never let him. I never had the courage to admit how I felt and he was always working on progressing his career. I didn't want to become a nuisance nor did I want to have him feel like he had to put what he was doing on hold. So I was just there, always in the background, waiting for him to see me in the shadows.

When that day came, it was on the tail end of something bad. He never talked about it, and I never pushed him, but I knew that something between him and Grif had happened. Something that they couldn't get past, which was how I became his roommate.

I thought that then maybe, just fucking finally, he might have a chance to see me.

Sadly, emotional blindness is something that is optional. Lawson had turned off any emotion other than being a brother toward me, until today.

I hear Lawson tell Bain that he shouldn't have kissed me.

"I'm being serious too, she's been in love with you for forever. You kissing her was the best choice you've made in a while. Now go home and kiss her some more so I can go kiss my woman. Don't know what your damn problem is."

I love you, Bain.

"I am not kissing her again. It was a mistake, and you're wrong: Jade isn't in love with me. I'm like her damn brother, family almost. She and I kissing will not happen again. I already asked her to forget it happened. She agreed. I just came over because I wasn't sure how to proceed," Lawson argues.

Yup, he sure did. Never wants to speak about it again with me but he can go tell everyone how it was such a mistake.

"You proceed with kissing her again, that girl is yours. She's right for you, dude. She puts up with your shit, never backs down. Takes care of your miserable ass, nurses you when you're sick, and does your damn laundry. She's practically your live-in wife already, the only thing you haven't done is consummated the marriage. Asking her to pretend it didn't happen is most likely only going to cause you hell," Bain fights for me.

He's right, of course, I do take care of Law, but it's not out of a sense of duty because I feel like he's my family. It's because I want to take care of him.

"She's not my wife. Roommates who are best friends take care of each other, that's all we are. She's someone's for sure, just not mine. What do you think's going to happen by pretending a kiss never happened?"

I'll never be anything to you, you've made Bain and I aware of it. Thanks.

I think about leaving, not listening to any more because I know the longer I stand here the more my heart is going to crack. Hearing him deny having any feelings for me has already lengthened the crack him kissing me put there.

"She's going to be hurt, that's for sure because she loves you. I've known it for years, don't know how you've ignored it, but I'm telling you, kissing her and then dismissing it like it was nothing just messed whatever you think you've got with her all up," Bain advises.

He's right, we can't go backward from here. It's only moving forward and over him if what he's saying to Bain is how he truly feels. I'll always care for him, deeply, and I will be his friend.

Lawson asks Bain how he can fix it.

I don't think you can, there's no fixing us if he really doesn't feel the same about me. I wouldn't be so hurt if I believed he felt nothing, if he hadn't kissed me tonight I would believe him. But I don't, I could feel how he felt in that kiss, that kiss was not nothing.

I deserve him to admit how he feels if he wants me. If he chooses to deny it, then no, there isn't any fixing to be done.

Bain replies that maybe I'll just be done with him, tired of waiting around for him to see me, and he's right, I am. He also says to give me space, which I don't think will help the final outcome either way. My mind's already made up, and hearing this conversation only solidifies my feelings on the matter.

Lawson pauses for a moment, probably deciding what he wants to do about me.

"Can I crash here?" Lawson asks Bain.

One night away isn't going to change anything.

"I'm not becoming an accomplice for your asshole behavior. You all just went out on a date. You left with your date, you not coming home looks like you stayed the night with that girl after kissing her. Asking her to forget the kiss you gave her, that will hurt her. Kissing her, asking her to forget it, then leaving with your date and not coming home. That shit won't just hurt her; it will break her heart. Go home, Law."

If I didn't happen upon them talking, I would've assumed he took Shay home.

"But maybe it would be easier to break her heart now, if you're right and she does have feelings for me. Maybe I should just hurt her now, save her the pain of thinking something can happen between us."

If he had taken Shay home, I would've hurt, but not as much as I do in this very moment. I was a fool to convince myself that kissing me had meant he really did have feelings for me, a complete and utter fool. I attempt to control the tears that fall down my face; I shouldn't be crying because I'm the cause of my hopes. My brain over-analyzes and overthinks because my heart just wants him.

"It's already happened, Lawson, it's *been* happening. Hurting her now or tomorrow or a week from now won't hurt her any less. You want to play blind? Go ahead, pretend that you've never felt her love. Pretend that you've never seen it. Pretend that you don't need it. But go pretend at your house."

My cue to run back to our apartment and lock myself in my room.

But I don't.

I stay frozen in front of the door.

Wanting Lawson to see me, wanting him to see that I did for him what he had already planned on doing to me.

He doesn't love me, if there were a chance for it to happen it would have by now. I'm not going to run home to pretend that I didn't hear everything he said only to walk on eggshells waiting to see how this will play out. See how he plans on breaking my heart himself.

I won't give him that.

"Night, Bain," Lawson says as he opens the door to find me standing there.

He freezes, something I had expected. He attempts to create words with his lips, but I stop him.

"You don't have to say anything, it's okay, I am okay." My hands shaking, I hide them behind my back so he doesn't see what a liar I am. "I heard everything, so I'll save you the task of trying to break my heart. It's already done."

With that, I walk away.

CHAPTER ELEVEN

Lawson

"Jade," I call out, my heart in my throat. I hadn't intended for her to overhear us. I didn't want her to hear how I felt like that in case what Bain had said was true.

When she runs into the apartment, I follow her.

"Jade, don't run away from me, from this. Let's talk about it."

"There's nothing more to say; I heard everything, and I think you made it pretty clear how you felt."

"I didn't mean to hurt you, that wasn't my intention. I went to Bain as a friend for advice on how to deal with this."

"You could've came to me. This was between us— you might not have wanted to hurt me, but you did. It's done, you've accomplished what you wanted. I saved you from having to figure out how to break my heart now just leave me alone."

"I'm not letting you run away from this, I'm coming to you now. Let's talk about this. You're my best friend—I can't just let you go to bed hurting and mad because of me. Let's fix this."

"You know what, I've had enough of this! I am exhausted, Lawson. I am so tired of hiding in the shadows. Bain was telling you the truth: I love you, I always have. I've been waiting for you to notice me, and when you finally do, it's only because you were caught up in being mad about my stupid job and about me being on a date with someone who works with me. You didn't kiss me because you wanted to, because you loved me. It was selfish of you to hurt me like that, Law, but you made me realize that you don't care and you never will. At least, not in the way that I do for you. I need to move on. I'll always be your friend, but I can't just hide how I feel anymore. It's killing me to do so, even if it's not returned, I just can't do this ..." She stops talking because she can't anymore—she breaks down crying.

I feel like an ass because I truly didn't believe Bain when he said she was in love with me, but I can't refute something when she actually tells me to my face that she loves me.

Even if I found the way to care for her, love her, even I know that it won't last. I'm not that person, I can't commit to anything more, and that's all on me. I don't have a sad story to tell about why I can't be with someone, it's just a risk I'm not willing to take. I refuse to put my entire heart and soul into a relationship that could end.

There's no way I would ever be that certain of anything, and I refuse to take that step; I won't ruin her or me.

But I want to take away the pain I've caused her.

I don't like being the reason she's crying. I hate that she's crying.

"Look at me," I demand of her.

I do the only thing I can think of to take her pain away, even if it only causes her more pain in the end.

CHAPTER TWELVE

Jada

"Look at me," he says.

I don't want to look at him. I'm embarrassed that I snapped, that I couldn't control myself and just lost my mouth filter. I wouldn't have said all that after hearing how he truly felt because it only makes me look more desperate.

I had to say it, though, had to make those feelings real to him.

Caught in-between running away to my room and looking at him, I realize that after tonight we will never be the same. This will be the last time I look into his eyes with love, because after tonight I'm bottling those feelings up and being done with it.

Our eyes clash, and I pour every ounce of my love into my stare. Wishing he could feel the same.

"Jade ..." Lawson whispers.

We stand face to face, my chest heaving from the exertion of spewing my heart out. Lawson stands with his arms at his sides, his thumbs running over his fingers in a nervous habit. I can't remember a time I've seen Lawson nervous, but I also can't recall a time that he's ever had someone confess their love for him.

"Lawson," I say his name. Silently questioning where we go from here.

He steps forward, closing in on me. I look down to the floor, his nearness making me nervous.

What's he doing?

What am I doing? I should go to my room now. End this.

"Don't hate me, please," Lawson says, his voice pained, like the idea of me hating him causes him pain.

"I couldn't ever hate you," I confess.

He steps closer, sliding his arms around my waist pulling me into him.

I know I should question him out loud, question what he's doing and why.

I'm selfish, though, so I don't. I don't care why he's doing this, even if it's the only time he ever pulls me close intimately. I should care, but I don't, even when it comes to protecting myself.

If this is the only time he'll ever share an intimate moment with me, I'll take advantage of it, to save as a memory for years to come.

He tips his head toward me, about to kiss me, and I meet him with my lips.

He glides one hand up my back and to my neck, holding my head while kissing me. His tongue swipes at my lips seeking permission to enter, and I allow him to.

He thrusts his tongue into my mouth, demanding my full attention—hard, rough, and passionately he takes me. I give it all back to him, demand he kiss me, demand he notice me now.

He pulls back for a moment groaning then lifts me and carries me to his bedroom.

This is happening.

It isn't a dream.

My feet hit the floor as he kicks the door closed behind him. He grabs my head and kisses me again, but this time slowly like he's savoring the feel and taste of me. I run my fingers over his shirt-covered chest, wanting to feel him without the fabric between us. I tug at the bottom of his shirt as a hint to take it off while he's kissing me.

He gets the hint, pulls back from me, and takes it off. Admiring his chest, I swipe my tongue over his right nipple. He groans huskily. I lick the left nipple, but he stops me to take ownership of my lips again.

We lose ourselves with each other to passion, stripping me as quickly as I strip him.

"Lay down on the bed, please."

I lie down, hoping he's coming to join me, but he has other ideas. Lawson grabs each knee and pulls my legs apart. He lies down, his elbows propping him up, and dives in between my legs.

I feel the flick of his tongue directly on my clitoris, swiping up and down before adding a finger to my entrance. My already wet center drips with need for him as he thrusts his finger inside of me while teasing my clit. I feel an orgasm taking over all too soon. "I'm going to cum," I moan out.

"That's what I want, I want to taste all of you," Lawson pauses in his ministrations to answer.

I combust, losing myself in the feeling of pleasure overtaking me. Pleasure received at the hands of Lawson. I long to return the favor but he's already taken control of what comes next.

Lawson slides over top of me, his lips meeting mine in a deep kiss. I can taste myself on his lips, and I shockingly don't mind. It only makes me want him more.

"I need you now," he says but doesn't move. Waiting for me to tell him I need him too.

"Yes," is all I manage to say before he wraps himself in a condom and thrusts into me.

I feel myself tense at the intrusion of Lawson's large size, but I become accustomed to it quickly. Feeling the tension, Lawson holds himself inside of me. "Are you okay? I'll stop," he asks worriedly.

"Keep going, I wouldn't be able to handle it if you stopped," I admit.

We can't end here.

Lawson pulls out of me and thrusts back in, picking up momentum. I grip into his sides with my hands, desperately holding on, wishing that this would last forever.

I reach for his lips with mine as I meet his thrusts. He kisses me longingly.

His thrusts become harder, deeper, more erratic, and I know that he's almost there. I'm there with him. Wrapping my legs around him, I can't help but whisper, "I love you," With one final slam of his hips, I break loose. Unlike my last orgasm, this one lasts for what seems like eternity. My entire body tenses and shakes while riding the wave of bliss.

At my finding release, Lawson finds his, groaning into my ear as he calls out my name.

Not wanting this moment to end, I clutch at his large frame, holding him on top of me and inside of me.

"I love you, I love you," I tell him over and over again.

CHAPTER THIRTEEN

Lawson

Running the pad of my fingertip along her lips, I linger on the corner of her mouth, a corner that's somehow remained upturned even while she's asleep. I take my time exploring her dimples, admiring how they are set into her skin. I run my fingers through her hair loving the vanilla scent that permeates the air. I take time being selfish because I know that once the light comes through those windows, when the sun has risen, I will lie to Jade.

I won't tell her that, yeah, maybe I do have feelings for her that go beyond some moral obligation to watch out for her as family.

I will lie because no matter what hope she has, it will never be enough for me to believe in us. For me to believe that I can have a relationship with anyone, even if it was her. She's convinced herself that because we've lived together for so long without huge arguments escalating to where one of us leaves that we can somehow have a long-term relationship that can go to that place called forever.

I'd like to think that forever exists.

It doesn't.

Forever is a place that's created by people with hopes and dreams of loving someone for their entire life. My hopes and dreams consist of only three things: running a successful gym, creating successful athletes, and being alone.

Jade isn't forever.

I am not her forever.

I just have to convince her that.

As the sun rises, I know Jade will be waking soon, so I put on some clothes and leave the room to make coffee in the kitchen. I know that I can't tell her what I'm about to tell her without being dressed.

Into my second cup of black coffee, I hear her stir. She makes her way to the bathroom then to the kitchen where I'm leaning against the counter preparing myself for what's about to come.

She approaches me with her heart in her eyes as she leans in for a kiss.

I give it to her.

One last final kiss, so I throw myself into it. I tell her I'm sorry with my lips, I tell her how much I wish that this could be different, how I wish I could see a relationship for us. How I wish I didn't have to reject her love.

I tell her all of that in seconds with my kiss.

Then I pull away.

"I can't."

Two, simple, cowardly words.

That's all I have to say for her to realize that I'm saying I can't do an *us*.

I can't be her forever, and she can't be mine.

She steels herself, stands tall, and whispers, "Okay."

JADE COMING SEPTEMBER 2016

ACKNOWLEDGEMENTS

Chad, my husband who always listens to my brainstorming for books, and urges me into my office to write. Who supports my traveling to events and even cooks dinner when I'm working. You are the best husband I could have asked for and an amazing father to our daughter I love you, forever and evers.

Payton, it has been an honor to be your mother. I get to watch you grow each day into a beautiful young lady. I see so much of myself in you, you got all of my bests and your fathers too. You are such a creatively imaginative wise soul; I love you Boog.

Tina, my best friend, who listens to me blab on and on about characters she has yet to meet in the form of words, you are the best, best friend and traveling assistant anyone could ask for. I see us growing old together.

Devin, if you hadn't introduced yourself to me I wouldn't have found my Lawson. You my dear are an absolute gentleman, with a kind soul. I am honored to call you my friend.

Twenty years ago

Lyrik,

i want you to move. i don't know why you're my neighbor but i don't want you to be. your hair is brown and brown is not pretty. please leave.

anson blake

Dear Anson Blake▨

Brown is very pretty you're just mean▨ I'm not moving▨ my parents said we can't▨ And what kind of name is Anson Blake anyway▨

Lyrik Everly

Lyrik everly,

anson blake is an awesome name, yours is not. just because you're my neighbor doesn't mean i'm going to be your friend.

not your friend,

anson blake

Dear Anson Blake

I don't want you to be my friend anyway

Lyrik Everly

Lyrik,

Fine.

anson blake

coming 2016

An excerpt from First Chance: Rock Romance #1

Natalie

"I think I just fell head over heels in love."

That's what my best friend Layla just squealed aloud to me.

She's staring at an album cover, drooling over the lead singer of a rock band I have never heard of. Don't get me wrong, I love music, I breathe music. It's a part of my soul. I just have no interest in a mainstream rock band- sell outs really. Layla tells me the band's name is Steele's Army; their lead singer Steele is her dream man. The man she would give everything up for. A man she would follow anywhere.

She mentions that they are coming to our college in Boston. Our college, the Berklee School of Music, entered some radio contest, and we won. I do not want to go but am preparing myself to. I know Layla is going to use the friend card to get me to agree to attend this sorry excuse of a concert. What's one night of putting up with shitty soulless music for my best friend?

I've known Layla my entire life. Our parents were best friends, until tragedy struck.

I hate remembering those days. It always hurts. We celebrated every birthday and holiday together as a family. Living across the street from each other our entire lives, our parents being so close to one another, we would have dinner together every night. As a family. Rotating who would host.

Until five years ago, Layla and I were staying at my house having a movie night while our parents went to a sit down fundraiser dinner raising money for abused children. Our parents were always supporting charities. They were fortunate to have money beyond their wildest dreams. I also donate quarterly, mainly to charities for children or music programs, in memoriam of them.

I still don't know all the details, nor do I want to. I think it would fuck me up even more if I did.

Recalling that night. It was late, way past our supposed bedtime, when we heard a knock at the door. I paused the movie we were watching and answered the door. It was a police officer. He introduced himself as Officer Petty's. He asked if I was Natalie Wright. That being me of course, I said yes. He then asked if Layla was there and if we would come with him.

I should have known something was wrong when he wouldn't tell us why we were on our way to the hospital. In fact, he wouldn't tell us anything at all. When you tell someone that their parents are deceased and that her best friend's parents are in surgery, you don't want them to be alone.

When we entered the ER he asked me if I wanted to see my parents' bodies, that's how we broke the crushing news. There was no way that I could handle something like that, and I really didn't wish to remember my parents that way, so I hastily declined.

Firstly, I was angered at the officer then at the doctors for not being able to save them. Then anger toward the cruelty of it all. What kind of person informs a fifteen-year-old that she is now alone in the world like that?

Later, I had found out that the officer did try to find out if I had any next of kin, preferring that they broke the news. I remember him asking if we would like to wait in the waiting room while Layla's parents were in surgery.

Where else would we have gone?

While we sat in that waiting room nervously awaiting news from the doctors on Layla's' parents condition, what was happening slowly sunk in. I became numb just feeling a wave of emptiness wash over me, my heart detaching itself from my emotions, no longer there. I was alone. They were my only blood family. My parents were both products of a one child family and my grandparents on both sides had passed way before I had made my way into this world.

Apparently our parents had a few drinks and thinking Layla's father was the least drunk, he drove them home. Speeding down the road, he lost control of the car causing the vehicle to crash into a guard rail, and my parents were then thrown from the car. EMTs found my parents' bodies about fifty feet away from the car. They were pronounced dead on the scene. Layla's father, Brian, was going at least seventy miles an hour and not one of them were wearing seatbelts.

Layla's father and mother recovered. They had scars from the injuries, easily hidden underneath clothing, but there was more scarring. Less visible to people that I could see in their eyes every time they looked at me for the past five years.

I think that's why they took over guardianship of me, out of obligation to my parents. I could have gone to a foster home. The money would have been put away in a trust, and when I turned eighteen I would have been discharged from the state and handed a loaded bank account.

I know they love me in their own way, but I also think the guilt ate at them so much that they did things out of both guilt and love. My parents were rich. Layla's were as well, and because of that my life was set. I never had to worry about anything. I could do whatever I wanted with my life. I chose to go to college many miles away from home. Away from the pity stares of everyone in my home town. With Layla.

We rented an apartment instead of residing in a dorm on campus. You never knew who you'd be rooming with, and we would rather be with each other. She's the only person who never treated me differently after my parents died. People think I should hate her. Hate her parents. How could I? They were all drinking, I'm sure it wasn't the first time they risked their lives seeing who could drive instead of calling a taxi or another friend. It could have been my parents driving.

Brian didn't mean for it to happen. It was an accident, a freak-forever life changing accident.

"Nat, NATALIE!" Layla's snapping fingers in front of my eyes and yelling at me.

She's telling me we have to go shopping for new outfits for this concert. I tell her she's buying since I don't even want to go in the first place. I must have spaced off thinking of the past. It doesn't happen often because I don't let it. I try to package it in a neat little box and shove it in the back of my mind.

I can afford it, but attending wasn't my idea, and I don't go around broadcasting the total in my bank account by spending it on frivolous materialistic items. I only spend money on necessities. Things I need to get by such as; college tuition, books, materials for class, shampoo, body wash, and food. I don't believe in luxuries because there are so many people in the Godforsaken world that aren't as well off as I am.

The first clothing store Layla sees we enter. It's not a high end shop, generally that's what Layla usually goes for. Always eager to buy the latest in designer brand clothing items. I walk around casually glancing at clothing racks. I look behind me to see if Layla has spotted anything of interest; she's looking at some purple mini-dress, which I know will be showing all of her worldly assets. There is no way I would be dressing like that. I'll take the comfortable t-shirt and jeans any day.

As Layla is in the dressing room, I start going through the sales racks, hoping to find a shirt with some kind of coverage. At about the tenth shirt, I have looked at I finally found the one. I pull it off the hanger; it's a vintage looking Tom Petty & The Heartbreakers 1978 Long After Dark tour t-shirt. It's ratty and tattered, but it's my style all the way.

Placing the now empty hanger back onto the clothing rack I go find Layla, she's standing in front of a mirror checking herself out. I too examine her. She's beautiful, not in the cheap I spent four hours doing my hair and make-up way. But the classic natural beauty. She doesn't need makeup, and her hair is always perfect long and black, reaching the middle of her back. Her beautifully tanned skin makes her features more noticeable, eyes that are an emerald green big and round shaped like almonds with long glorious eyelashes anyone would be jealous over. A small nose and high cheekbones, her mouth pink and pouty and she's a size two with close to no curves.

She doesn't need anything artificial to make her beauty stand out.

Needless to say, we are polar opposites. I look at myself in the mirror over her shoulder; I never wear make-up on my pale face. I have never seen the need to, and I have no interest in calling attention to myself. I threw my hair up in a big scraggly bun; I have pieces of hair sprouting out all over. It's a golden brown, curly with a hint of frizz and long, it reaches the top of my ass. I have round rosebud color lips and my small nose has a slight bridge, drawing my coppery brown eyes out. Size two I am not, I have wide hips and curvy love handles.

I'm not noticeable, and I plan to keep it that way.

Layla has decided on the purple mini-dress. I glance up, thanking the stars in a whisper. I was counting on spending at least two hours in here before she had made her mind up. The mini-dress is more a piece of cloth just there to cover the actual intimate body parts, but enough for anyone to make out exactly what she is hiding.

Thinking of the shirt I chose, I happen to have a kick ass pair of jeans in my closet to go with it. I will never understand people like my best friend Layla. Why would you want to spend all night at a concert in uncomfortable clothes, a chance with the band? So not worth it to me.

She's going on and on about Steele, apparently he came from nothing, the started a band and BAM! Rock-star of the charts...I drown her out. I have no care for a band who makes their money by selling bad boy images and sex, making mediocre music that means absolutely nothing.

I believe a song should touch you. Glide over your spine inducing goosebumps, with your heart pounding to the beat. Possibly bring tears to your eyes just by feeling the words. Or make you smile and set your mood for the day ahead. That is music that I listen to that I am a true fan of.

Music that I can only dream of making. Growing up, my dad listened to all the greats. Making me fall in love with them, as well. It's something I've carried with me, and I will always hold onto. It didn't matter where we were. With my dad, he was always playing music or humming a tune to a great song aloud. He is the reason why I decided to major in music.

An excerpt from Last Chance: Rock Romance #2

Prologue

Layla

Just getting off from my eight-hour shift at the hippest local bar in Boston, I am exhausted and ready to hit my bed full force. Luckily I had a day shift, so it wasn't nearly as busy as it is when working the night shift. I can't get Nat out of my mind. In the past week, I have only heard from her once.

When I dropped her off, she promised me, she would stay in contact. This is the longest we will be away from each other since we've been alive. I also know this is a way out of her comfort zone. The members of "Steele's Army" are daunting, and I know she puts on that tough exterior act, but she can only hold that facade up for so long.

I couldn't help but push her into this. After five years of seeing her live her life hidden beneath this shell, as her best friend, I refused to stop being her enabler. She ought to have so much more than what life has thrown at her, forced upon her. I know my parents; my father more so, feels extreme guilt.

I also know that since the tragedy Nat has never blamed my dad. I have never needed her confirmation; we have always been a family. The accident ruined my dad. He killed his best friend, his brother and his wife.

After that day, he could never keep eye contact with me; a big part of the reason I agreed and supported Nat's decision to leave New York. I was tired of my family not being able to linger around me for more than ten minutes. They thought that money could somehow substitute their absence.

Do I enjoy the money? Is it cold in Antarctica?

I enjoy not having to rely on student grants or loans to pay for college. I also enjoy not having to wonder where my next paycheck is going to come from, and worry over how each bill will get paid. I like being able to help people, others that are not as fortunate as I.

I enter the apartment throwing my car keys down on the kitchen counter, too lazy to attempt at cooking something to eat, I throw ramen in the microwave. While my food is cooking, I decide to go into Natalie's room. This week has been agony for me. Being without her here in this apartment isn't the same. It's lonely without her music jamming loudly at all hours of the day, hell it's just lonely without her.

I have probably slept in her room four nights this week. Finding comfort by enfolding myself in her blankets. Our lives were planned to be intertwined long before we were born. Natalie will always be my other half. A part of my being. She has always felt that I was her sanity, her reason to keep moving every day. She's always voiced her opinion on that.

What she doesn't know is that I feel an overbearing guilt at what my father did. Accident or no. If my dad had just suggested they call a taxi, her parents would still be here. She wouldn't be as closed off as she is now. She wouldn't be severely heartbroken trudging along in life. Sometimes I think she can see through me. See why I do what I do. She puts on the hard shell to her exterior never letting anyone but me in. I do the opposite. I have let people in all the time. But only for a few nights of fun. Those few nights allow me to feel alive again. But I am not deserving of feeling alive.

So when the guilt makes its way in, slowly creeping along my soul. That's when I kick them out of my bed. To be honest, they don't deserve it either. If I let someone in, and let them know how much I ache for Natalie, how much hate and disgust I have for my parents, or how much these thoughts consume me, they would only look at me with indifference. No one could or would ever understand.

I open her bedroom door and straight away notice she's laying in her bed.

What the fuck?

Why is she here in her room?

She should be on a tour bus right now. How the hell did she get here?

I walk over to her bed and start shaking her awake. She doesn't respond. I shake her again, this time a little harder.

"Nat!" I yell out.

"Natalie!"

Her not responding to me has my stomaching overturning. To set my mind at rest, I lay my head on her chest, just to hear her heartbeat. It's beating, slowly. I start screaming her name out loud. Hoping, no praying that she will answer me or make some kind of movement. Her face is abnormally pale

I jump off the bed and yank my cellphone out of my pocket, furiously dialing 911. Natalie what did you do? The dispatcher answers the call. Rushing the words out I tell her my friend is laying in her bed, not responding to anything I do and that her heart is barely beating. She tells me she's sending an ambulance. That everything will be all right.

Right now I am having a very hard time accepting that everything will be okay. I have never seen Natalie like this.

What happened?

As the dispatcher is still on the phone, she directs me to check Nat's pulse. To keep checking it to make sure she hasn't stopped breathing altogether. Sitting on the bed beside Natalie's body with my thumb on her wrist, I glance at her nightstand and notice a piece of paper sitting there.

A letter. Addressed to me. Oh Natalie. She did this on purpose.

An excerpt from Find Me: Rock Romance #3

Chapter 1

Liam

The Queen, as I have now dubbed her, had her Princess last night. I think the last time that I can remember seeing Ryan this happy, was the day that we got signed. Temperance, a beautiful name and fitting for one so innocent and small. She is the spitting image of her mother, only she has Ryan's blue eyes.

Before Layla and I left last night, we got to hold her for a bit. I was nervous as hell, because I never once had a chance to hold such a tiny baby. Thought I would drop her, but with Natalie's urging and confidence, I picked her up. I cuddled her to my chest and held on tightly.

We stayed for a few hours, all the while I was inconsiderately selfish with Temp, not even wanting her own parents to hold her. The Queen and I shared a bond. I don't know why, or even how, but we did, and that bond carried on to her newly born child. I was jealous that Ryan got to be with her and have a family.

I wanted what he had.

I wanted to take care of her.

Forever.

My body, my emotions, owned her and she me. But when it came time to leave, I kissed Temperance on the forehead and laid her in her father's arms and walked away. I gulped in the stale air around me, swallowing my emotions. I hid my inner turmoil of jealousy well. But not well enough.

"We're going to let you both get some rest, we'll come visit in the morning." I say, glancing between Ryan and Natalie, who are snuggled together on the hospital bed with Temperance laying on Natalie's chest. I take a step closer to them, almost begging for the punishment of having to feel the emotions of longing and loneliness taking over my heart.

I am my own worst enemy.

I take another step closer to Natalie's side. I look down at the beautiful baby girl and then back into her mother's eyes. "You did well. Queen." I whisper. Then place a chaste kiss upon her cheek. I stand upright and notice Ryan giving me a furiously questioning stare, but I ignore him and his unspoken questions. Questions that I don't want to answer. I turn around and walk away.

Natalie doesn't know it yet, but seeing her and Ryan laid together as a family upon that bed made the decision for me. To cut this bond and walk away. I can be her friend, but not her best friend. I can't be that close. It wouldn't be fair to Ryan, I, or her, and especially not Princess.

I make it back to the waiting room, when I am confronted by the guys. Gage, Jason, and Zepp all stand up to greet me. I had called them as soon as Ryan had called me, to let them know that the baby was coming. I suggested they wait until the morning to visit. Thankful that they had not listened.

I don't want to have this conversation right now. All I want to do is get in my car and drive back to what used to be Layla and Natalie's apartment, but is now mine and Layla's apartment. When Natalie moved in with Ryan, I took her old room out of convenience. Layla didn't need a roommate to help with bills, but I couldn't let her live alone and if I were to be honest with myself, I wanted- no needed something to hold onto of Natalie's at the time.

We have canceled the tour until later next year and Ryan installed a studio in the basement of his house, so we could all conveniently work out of his house and I refused to room there as the other guys did. I knew I didn't want to put any roots down in Boston. As much as my heart yearned to be close to Natalie, I knew that there would come a time that I had to cut myself off from her due to my having an interest that's more than friendly. I just didn't think it would have been so soon. That it would have had to be now.

"Well aren't you going to tell us how she's doing?" Gage interrupts my thoughts.

I hesitate. I would rather be anywhere else at this moment. These guys have the power to read right through me. I can try to hide my emotions all I want, but they will always see right through it. Effortlessly.

What am I supposed to say? "She's beautiful, the baby I mean." I stumble with my words. "She looks just like her mother, they're still exhausted, but I'm sure if you guys were to peek in for a few minutes, they wouldn't care." I walk away awkwardly, unsure of what else to say. I don't want their questions, and they are one hell of a nosy bunch.

I exit the waiting room and make my way to my car, when Layla starts talking. I forgot that she was with me or that I was her ride.

"What is your problem?" She asks.

"Nothing. I'm fine. Maybe tired." I reply dismissively, while getting in the car.

She lets out a sigh, exasperated with my short answers. Since I started staying with her and Natalie, she has done nothing but give me hassle about my feelings for Nat. I tried like hell to tame my shit down toward Nat. I always knew that she belonged to Ryan, much to my regret.

But I couldn't help how I felt. I tried and tried. The more time I spent with her, trying to help her heal, watching over her, the more my feelings grew. The pregnancy was just fuel added to the flame on the torch I had already begun carrying for her. I knew she wasn't ready and even though it made me a shit ass best friend to Ryan, I could not help it. As the saying goes, the heart wants what the heart wants.

An excerpt from Forever, Hold On: Rock Romance #5

Chapter One

Jason

"Welcome to our humble abode." I say while unlocking the door to our house. Gage, Zepp and I bought a house together, just outside of Los Angeles years ago, when we each got our share of the sign-on check our label paid us. About an hour drive from Ryan's condo on the beach. Thanks to Ryan and Abby, we were allowed a two week break during the tour. Natalie having Temperance is what gave us favor to receive two weeks off. We all decided to head back to California for the break. It helped that we were all in the same area when the break ended, and Ryan had some affairs to put in order, so California was ideal.

I figured I would see my family while we were here, along with Zepp's and Gage would continue working on his newfound relationship with Abby. She's staying with us during the duration of our mini vacation.

"Your home is beautiful." Abagail says, leaving her jaw slack, causing her mouth to hold open on the last word.

She's in awe. I'll have to admit it is pretty nice, for a bachelor's pad. We all agreed that it was the one, when we first viewed it. We had looked at a few other houses before this one, but none of them came up to par, as this one did.

"How many bedrooms are in this place?" Abby asks.

"Six. Three are guest rooms." Gage answers for me.

"Why so many bedrooms? There's only three of you." she questions.

"Abagail, when we're home, people stay over often. It's convenient to have an extra bed for the person to sleep in. Or in my case, maybe the person you plan on sleeping with is only around for the one night. You don't want to take her back to your own bed. The guest rooms work out perfectly." I explain.

"Oh." she says while glaring at Gage.

"Gage never uses the rooms; in case you're wondering." I interject before she says something she could come to regret, in defense of Gage.

"Let me give you a tour, ending with my room." Gage says to her sweetly.

The pang of jealousy hits me. Not jealousy because I have a thing for Abagail, because I don't. Jealousy as in Gage has finally found that happiness.

Happiness that I've been looking for, happiness that has seemed to escape me, and that I don't believe I'll ever find. I've tried lowering my expectations. I've long since faced the reality that I won't ever find love like my parents have, true soul completing love. Love that Gage, Liam, and Ryan have found.

When women look at me, it's not with pure intentions of true love and lifelong happiness. It's instant-love, unreal and deranged, eyes filled with lust for rock stars. It has nothing to do with me, but who I am. Something each one of us in Steele's Army has dealt with. We've all ridden the fence of crazy, causing mistrust and misguidance, when it comes to finding what we long for.

Love and happiness, to replace the loneliness of a cold bed and an empty heart.

Abagail and Gage make their way back to me, before ending the tour in their bedroom. "I was thinking that maybe I would call my friends and invite them out for a week. If that's okay with you and Zepp. Gage already said he had no problem with it." Abagail says to me.

I mind if she has friends over as much as I mind the guys having people over, not at all.

"No problems here, and I doubt Zepp would mind either. Make the call. I'll book them flights if you'd like, just get me their information."

"Are you sure? You would do that for me?" she asks, smiling.

"Of course." She flings her arms around me and pulls me in for a hug.

What's with these girls and their touching? Natalie, Layla, and now Abagail too. As soon as they fall in love, it's like they become emotional basket cases when it comes to touching. Angry, sad, joyous, excited, they immediately touch to express what they're feeling and their partner's don't seem to mind it either. I would rather Gage get upset, maybe jealous over it, to prevent the touching.

But it seems as if he encourages it. He knows that I have boundaries with anyone touching me and he enjoys my uneasiness when it comes to another's hand on my body, innocent or not.

Asshole.

I give him a knowing glare, that I'm aware he enjoys this shit. He winks at me. I slowly pry Abagail's hands off me, "Not a problem. Like I said, just get me the information and I'll book it."

"I'll call Selena now. Thank you." she says, smiling.

I make my escape into the kitchen.

It's not that I've had some tragic thing happen in my past with touching, no one's abused me or anything. It's that because of what I do, what we do as a profession, everyone always feels like they have a right to reach out and grab me. Pull me in for a hug, kiss my face, often grabbing my ass. If they were to ask me for a hug, I wouldn't have such an issue with it. Then I would know to expect the touching. Instead, it's forced upon me and I don't like it.

"I got ahold of Selena, she's going to call Raven and they'll fly out as soon as you can get them an available flight." Selena informs me.

I'm sprawled out on the chase that's part of the large black sectional we have in our living room, one foot dangling off the edge and my laptop laying above me. "I was just searching flights; I can get them a red-eye today if that's what you want. I mean if you think they can pack fast enough, I can even have a car pick them up and drive them to the airport to save time."

"Really Jason? That's so sweet of you, they'll be fine with whatever you can get. I'll make sure of that."

"All right then. I'll call the airline to book it, even get them in first class. It'll make for an easier flight."

"Thank you, normally they would drive out wherever I was if they could. Shows or stops I'd make that weren't far away, they'd join me at. I can't thank you enough." she says while I sit my laptop to my side and pull my cellphone out to make the call.

"As long as Gage is happy, that's enough thanks. I couldn't repay you, for being that for him."

"You'll find your happiness to Jason, it could be sooner than you think, but it will happen. You're too good of a catch for it not to."

"Yeah, yeah, enough of this emotional stuff you're wearing me out." I tell her.

"Fine. I'll let you call and arrange the tickets, let me know so I can call Selena back with the information."

"Will do Abby."

An excerpt from Letting Go: Rock Romance #6

Chapter One

Zepp

Blinded by the sun, I place my hand on my forehead blocking the bright rays shining into my eyes so I can see her, Rush, my sister. My parents were born in the early sixties, teens by the seventies and shared a passion for rock music, ironically meeting at a concert and falling in love.

As you can tell, so the story goes, that when I was conceived many, many years later in the nineties that's what my parents were still listening to. Embarrassingly so they once told me of how my name came to be Zeppelin, after Led Zeppelin. Stairway to heaven was playing in the background on the night I was most likely conceived, and Tom Sawyer on the night Rush was most likely conceived.

They weren't creative, they could have chosen a band member to name us after, but no, they chose the entire band.

Rush is four years younger than I, at only eight. We're on a family vacation in Myrtle Beach, South Carolina.

Choosing to stay in bed a little longer, my parents gave Rush and I permission to walk along the ocean, located behind our hotel. It's not even noon and the humidity has hit its peak, and the ocean is packed with beach goers.

"Zepp, I want to go swimming." Rush comes running up to me shouting with excitement.

"Mom said we couldn't, remember that's the only reason they let us come down. We have to wait until they're with us."

"Oh, come on don't spoil all the fun, just a quick dip. It's hot and I'm starting to sweat, I won't tell. I promise, pinky promise." She holds her pinky out to mine and pouts.

She knows I'm a sucker for the pouty face. I'm the big brother, always protecting and spoiling.

"Fine, but only for a few minutes, that way we can dry before going back upstairs."

"Yes!" she shouts while kicking her sandals off.

I find a place to throw my shirt on the sand where no one else will be walking over it. Rush adds her clothes too and soon we're bathing in cold ocean water.

"We can't go out that far. Don't let the water go past your knees, Rush."

What was supposed to be only a few minutes turns into longer, maybe an hour. We take turns running away from the wave's right onto the sand of the beach, seeing who could outrun the waves the best.

Eventually she cons me into letting her bury me beneath the sand, we borrow another kid's shovel and she starts to dig. I use my hands to help make a shallow hole, big enough for my body to be buried in.

"Okay, help me get out of here."

"Nope. Get out of it yourself." Rush walks away, close to the edge of the ocean allowing the water to pool at her feet. I yell to her, "Rush, help me out of this." She turns toward me and laughs, the quickly runs away.

I try twisting my arms and kicking my feet in the sand that's currently holding me hostage, and not wanting to budge. I squint my eyes and search for Rush to no avail. With the mass of people playing in the water, I can't find her.

A kid walks by me and I ask for help. As he digs me out, the dirt becomes loose enough for me to move my limbs around and free myself. That's when I hear it.

A loud and aching cry from a woman. "Help! Help! She's drowning!"

I follow the voice, telling myself that there's no way it could be Rush, she knows better, she knows not to go out that far, and that the ocean is dangerous and unrelenting.

I find the woman who is still screaming. She's holding herself, crying in fear. Fear for the drowning victim. There's three men trying to reach the victim in time, before the ocean claims another life. All I can see is hands smacking at the water with force, they disappear and then reappear as the waves roll. Until I don't see the hands any longer.

And all I can think is it can't be Rush.

The hands disappear for minutes, but one of the guys finds them and tows those small hands back to shore.

Its Rush.

I jump, awakened by my alarm, thank God. Tears are pooling at my eyes. I swipe them away before tossing my blanket off the bed. Sitting up, I walk over to the bathroom and flick the light on. It takes a moment for my eyes to adjust to the brightness, but when it does, I stare at myself in the mirror.

I always wonder if others can see the pain hidden in the depths of me, if I'm easily read. This dream, a nightmare in reality, and in truth comes every year, right around this time. In the weeks, the days following the date of the event that really did take place.

The day Rush drowned, the day I couldn't help her, the day I let her wander away from me. The day that crushed my parents, stole their dreams never to be found, the day I was in charge of my younger sister and I allowed her to swim in the ocean. All because of a pouty face and a pinky promise, something so juvenile even for me at age twelve.

Brown eyes scrunched up in sadness, pink lips puckered in a pout. A look she made all the time, holding me under her thumb. A look I'll never see her express.

Rush didn't die that day, no, she was saved, by a stranger that was later to become a hero in my eyes. I threw accountability on myself and him, even my parents for letting us go outside without them that day, I made us responsible for what happened to Rush.

Do you know what happens to people who lose oxygen for that amount of time? Cerebral Anoxia, that's what doctors call it, decreased oxygen in the brain. It can be as little as three minutes and brain damage is imminent. Doctor's predicted that oxygen was nonexistent for seven minutes.

Rush is alive, no longer the person she was or could have become. Without oxygen, brain cells die, and that's what happened to Rush. She endured massive brain damage, she was in a coma for six weeks after that. Four of which we stayed in South Carolina, until it was safe enough for her to be flown by medical helicopter back home. When she finally awoke, two weeks after, she woke in a vegetative state. My hope for her survival dwindled, down to nothing. My parent's eyes were full of regret, and anger toward me.

Nothing short of a miracle, she came out of the vegetative state a week later, but she wasn't the same. When she woke, they ran MRI's and CT scans to monitor her brain and its healing process, she sustained brain damage because of the incident. Rush has long-term memory loss, she had to learn how to speak again and walk, she had to learn how to do everything that an eight-year-old should know how to do, some things she couldn't latch on to right away. She speaks slowly, and has trouble walking still. She'll never be allowed to live on her own, she can't care for herself, nor does she have the possibility of ever having her own independent life.

She lost everything, within minutes, she lost her future.

Today is the day, fourteen years ago, Rush's future was ripped away, because of a decision I made. The nightmare always comes back, the reality of what happened and what I could've done to make the outcome not be what it is. Music is my escape from life. Escape from every situation I've had to deal with, escape from Rush herself, from my parents. Escaping the guilt that it wasn't me who had drowned.

An Excerpt from Stolen; In My Blood

The End.

June 26th 2014

Survivor.

Sur-vive verb \sər-'vīv\

: To remain alive: to continue to live

: To continue to exist

: To remain alive after the death of (someone)

That's what they all tell me I am. Eight different psychologists, four police officers, two doctors and my mother are all convinced that I now belong in the category of a survivor. Although, I strongly believe the definition is sorely lacking, it's more of a stereotype for people who were lucky enough to live through unfortunate events or circumstances. The word survivor doesn't seem sufficient. It's too simple, also insipid. Sometimes, there are words that just feel right on your tongue; they describe something monumental without even trying. I roll my eyes at every single person who has sat down with me believing that they would pick my brain and know all the answers. That they could diagnose me with some easily labeled condition, they could fix me with a few pills that I could swallow every day by mouth. There is no fixing me.

Just because I'm alive should by no means make me the definition of survivor. I'm breathing. My body is pumping blood; all of my limbs can move with functionality and limber. Sure, I'm alive after everything that has happened in the last year. However, it does not in any way mean that I survived. My body may be intact. No appendages are missing, not that it wasn't threatened, but my mind is shattered. One year-ago today I was college bound and lost in a bliss of naiveté. I believed myself to be as strong as steel, I could carry the weight of the world on my shoulders without an issue. I lived in a world of make believe, where there were only kindness and caring, where every single dream, I ever had would come true.

That's what I remember about the shadow of myself, of who I used to be. The guileless princess who was oblivious to the ways of the world. Now, I'm a shell of my former self. Lost and broken, not only because of the events that occurred, but also because of him. If he hadn't set the plan in motion to steal me from my home, to follow another's orders, I would be alive. My mind is a sea full of turbulent waves. My thoughts are undetermined currents moving nowhere fast, and only memories that I can bring to the forefront of my mind are the ones I would wholeheartedly like to forget first.

Abducted.

Ab-duct verb \ab-ˈdəkt, əb-; 2 also ˈab-ˌ\

: To seize and take away (as a person) by force

: To draw or spread away (as a limb or the fingers) from a position near or parallel to the median axis of the body or from the axis of a limb

That's what I was one-year abducted, kidnapped, captured, snatched, or stolen, any way you look at it. That's what I was. Fifteen days, ten hours and thirty-seven minutes is how long I have been free. Free from his hold. No longer being threatened or held against my will. Not that I have fully convinced myself yet, that in the end, he was ever holding me without a choice. Had I asked would he have let me go? It's a question I've asked myself at least once an hour since I made it home.

At some point along the way during my abduction I stopped fighting. Maybe it was because I lost hope that I would ever escape their clutch. The flame on the torch of hope I carried went out. Eventually, I just gave in to every single demand. I caved because at some point, I became wanted, and someone needed me other than my mother. I felt like I finally found a reason for just being. I'm still unsure of how everything ended up happening the way it did.

Was this what he had planned for? Did he know that this would happen? Did he know that in the end, I would break? That not having him would leave me empty inside, that I wouldn't be able to sleep without his body lying next to mine? Did he know that I would mourn the loss of him?

All questions that I would never have a chance at getting the answer to. Questions I'm not sure I deserve to be answered.

My mother has been towing me around to different doctors' offices. Saying that they can repair me, that I can be healed. What she doesn't know, what I won't ever tell her, is that I can't be mended. There is no recovery for me. I'm undeserving of a cure. I'm not the same person I was when she last saw me. A lot of shit can happen to a person in a year, horrible shit, things that I will never repeat to another soul.

I was Aura.

No longer do I have an identity. I, a nameless murder.

An Excerpt from Broken; In My Blood

Mission: Freedom.

July 3rd 2013

Today is the day I set my plan in motion. No one else around here plans on seeing reason, that what is happening is vicious and nauseating. On top of being immoral and just wrong. Everyone is on my father's payroll and simply goes along with whatever he says. I plan on changing that though.

My father wants a daughter to take over his empire, all right. I'll do what he wants, but what he won't know is that I plan on changing what it is that he's is doing here. I'm going to free every woman he has locked in that warehouse and any others that come along.

What I have to do though, is get on his good side. Convince Cruz and him that I am in on this one hundred percent. It's going to kill me, and I am praying to any and all Gods above that I can make it through this unscathed. I've been awake most of the night thinking on how I might be able to do this. All I know is that I will have to do whatever he asks of me to be able to fully convince him of my sincerity. He'll see through lies, he will see through me if I second guess any of his actions.

A loud bang goes off outside of my room, causing me to jump up out of bed. What in the fuck was that? My door swings open and I come face to face with my father's right hand man, Cruz. Normally, under very different circumstances I would be attracted to him. Hell, I was attracted to him when he was just a customer in Irene's Deli. Now I can't think of him without thinking about him kidnapping me, about him tying me up or him helping my father sell women.

Repulsion ripples through me, causing me to gag. I quickly place my hand over my mouth, an attempt to stop what I ate previously that night form coming up. I have to find a way to be stronger. To overcome this. If I were to retch every time my father mentions what he does, or if for some reason I have to reenter that warehouse for anything other than rescuing those women and I end up vomiting then my father will know that I'm only being traitorous and thwarting his end goal.

"Are you going to be sick?" Cruz asks while placing his hand on my lower back.

I pull myself out of his grip. "I'm just fine. Do you have a reason to be here?"

"No need to be so rude. I saw your face pale, you looked like you were going to be sick. Not that it matters now as you seem to be fine. He wants to see you."

An Excerpt from Savior; In My Blood

The End.

June 26th 2014

Aura cannot find out that I'm alive, if she does it won't bode well for her. She wouldn't be safe like she is now; her mother wouldn't be safe. Many people would be out to get her, not just our government but many horrendous people, clients, of her fathers. Previous clients. They would kill her without hesitation and I am the only living link to her, if she's with me, they get her. It's better for me to keep them off track, for the previous clients to follow me across the world and back, believing I know where she is in hiding.

Although she isn't in hiding but in plain sight, just irrevocably changed. Changed because of my actions, Guillermo's actions, his selfish wants. She isn't the Aura that I kidnapped a year ago, the same innocent soul I met then. She's grown harsh to the world and with good reason. No matter how much I tried to keep her safe, to keep her naïve and protect her, in the end I couldn't accomplish the impossible. I broke her down, tarnished her heart and ripped her soul apart. I'm undeserving to be forgiven, not by her, her mother of even God. When judgment day comes down upon me, it's something I would gladly repent for throughout eternity. Ultimately, that's exactly what I deserve.

An Excerpt from Beautiful Beast #1

Prologue

"As I have said, you have no reason to trust me, and an excellent reason not to."

-Robin McKinley, Beauty

Two loud thuds sound on my bedroom door, "Sweetie," My mom says as she welcomes herself in without my greeting. "Today's a big day for you, think you'd like to get up? Help me finish loading the car, please."

"Sure thing Stella." I reply shortly.

"Lily, you wanted this. Dad and I are only making you see it through. When you commit to something- you do it. You can hardly be mad at us for wanting you to get a college education."

"I wanted this before everything happened. You know that. Forcing me to go isn't going to help any. Plus, Dad's not even here"

She sighs. "Well it's done. Tuition has been paid and your bags have been packed. You're going to see this to the end. Your father wanted to be here, he told me so himself. So get out of that bed and get dressed, breakfast is already getting cold on the table. You leave in one hour."

She makes her way back to the door, "Lily, just try this please. Three months is all I ask. If you feel that after three months you can't do it anymore I will come get you myself. Okay?"

"Yup."

When I'm finally showered and dressed I make my way downstairs to the kitchen table where mom has already served breakfast. "Banana pancakes and bacon, your favorite. Eat up so you have a full stomach for your long drive ahead."

I mumble a thanks and begin eating when mom interrupts my angry thoughts, infuriated that she's making me go there, even if I had suggested it in the first place.

I recommended it when I had hope that there was a surgery to make my face look somewhat normal. When I thought I wouldn't look like a scarred beast, now that we know that it's impossible I want to just stay home and hide myself away. Last month I found a house where I could rent my own room that wasn't on campus, less of an obligation to mingle with other students; less of a chance that anyone would see my face.

The room was mine, I got it and paid up on the rent. My mom took out a second mortgage on the house and paid my two-year tuition in full. Not that they could afford it. I knew that my mom was going to have to trade her newer Durango in for a smaller cheaper midsize car, to lower her monthly payments. I also know that mom has taken on a second job; working from home to obtain extra income.

My medical bills are in the high six figures, and they've only been getting higher with every single appointment in hopes that I would get a new face.

All that money wasted, on hope.

Guilt eats at knowing my parents can't look at my scarred face without flinching, that no one can look at my face without flinching, or gagging.

My friends left me behind when they saw what the accident caused, the fleshy ridges of newly healed scars, skin that was torn off the right side of my face. I only have my parents and look at where I've put them.

In the fucking poor house.

"Lily Lotus. My Lily Lotus. Have you ever wondered why your father and I chose to name you after two flowers?"

"You liked flowers?" I shrug my shoulders.

"That too, but no not because I liked flowers. But because of the meaning and symbolism behind each flower. When we saw you for the first time, holding you in our arms, we knew that nothing but Lily Lotus would be good enough for you."

"I never knew that. I still think it's a silly name." Although after spending 19 years with the name I've gotten used to it and have come to acceptance, even after the constant badgering from fellow schoolmates about my name. I've come to terms with being named after a flower.

"Well how about I tell you the meaning behind your name, and then you can reevaluate if you think it's so silly."

"Okay." I say in agreement, while placing my dirty dishes in the sink. I'd rather a nice conversation be what I leave her with, this closeness, this talking, instead of arguing or silence- how we usually communicate. Our closeness, our mother and daughter bond having disappeared over the last ten months.

"Have a seat."

I sit in the chair next to her, and listen.

"Lily means pure, and that you were. Innocent and pure and beautiful, as much as you don't believe it LL, you still are. There's a Greek mythological story involving a Lily too, it's a little odd for a story- but it also means motherhood. Something I hoped one day you would achieve for yourself, when the time is right of course and you found the love of your life. The myth of the story involves the making of the Milky Way as well, and well I will leave that one for you to read yourself. As odd as it is, it's a touching story and it just fit. The pureness inside of you could be seen and felt by your father and I, you were a white light LL. It fit you then as much as it does today."

"What about Lotus, mom?" I interrupt, as I can see she's getting emotional about my own insecurities. Another reason I can't stay here any longer as much as it pains me, and as much as I don't want to go and I'm fighting it- I know that my own issues with myself are affecting them too.

"Lotus...a beautiful flower. Did you know that a lotus begins growing in dark dirty dinger water, only to emerge in three days and bloom above the darkness that is a dirty pond? Lotus means rebirth, its flower retracts during the night only to emerge the following day, every day after, rising above adversity. Adversity to its living conditions, the mud and dirt below the surface. Only to bloom a bright and beautiful flower each day. LL, you too can rise above any and all adversity. It doesn't matter what dirt you've stepped in, what mud you've fought through or how deep the water was in which you've drowned. You can rise above it all- if you would just believe in yourself. Once upon a time you did. You have that confidence; you possess that courage. I know the accident has robbed you of that- of many things. But I can only hope, as your mother, as the one whom created and carried your life inside, that you will rise above again."

I swipe my hands at the tears flowing gently down my cheeks, she is always seeing the best in me, and remaining positive for my future even after all that has happened to me- has happened to us.

"Hopefully mom." I say to appease her worries. I know that if I were to leave today with an image that I won't survive, that I won't be strong enough to do this on my own- she'll be left with monumental worry. I can't willingly leave her knowing that.

"I'll be fine, and maybe- just maybe I'll find my way back to the person I used to be." She stands up as I do and pulls me in for a hug.

"Your father wanted to be here to say goodbye, he really did but he had an early day. He told me to tell you that he loves you and that we'll be in town to see you the weekend before Thanksgiving. I love you LL, call me when you get there so I know you made it safely. Make sure to call us if you need anything at all- Oh and check in every week. I know that college life can be crazy and all, but please check in with us." Mom rambles as I kiss her goodbye on her cheek.

I see the tears in her eyes threatening to fall so I back away and start laughing, "Yeah, yeah, yeah Mom. I don't think you'll have to worry about me not checking in. I doubt I'll be too busy for you. I'll call when I make it to the house so you can stop worrying that they're murders or something. I love you, Mom."

With those last words I depart, leaving her in the kitchen. My car was packed last night so all I would have to do was eat and hit the road bright and early.

I shut the front door quietly, only to get in my car and have to slam the rusty door shut a few times before the locking mechanism actually catches and keeps the door shut.

I adjust the rearview mirror, mom having driven it yesterday causes my view to be the roof of my car. I turn the keys in the ignition while pressing on the gas a couple of times before it starts, throw my Mumford & Sons C.D.

into the ancient disc player in my car and put the car in drive.

To new beginnings.

ABOUT THE AUTHOR

A.L. Wood resides in Queensbury, NY with her husband and daughter. When she's not writing she's reading and spending time with her family and friends.

A.L. Wood can be found on Facebook and twitter, both links are below if you are interested in keeping up with any new releases.

https://www.facebook.com/ALWood

https://twitter.com/ALWoodAuthor

63027828R00085

Made in the USA
Charleston, SC
26 October 2016